CHRISGOPHER COLUMBUS ™

in

STOWAWAY ON THE SANTA MARIA

Dedicated to Britain Cecil

Written by Terry and Barbara Cecil
Illustrated by Steve Smallwood/The Ivy League of Artists, Inc.

Infiniti, Inc. will donate 10% of the wholesale cost of each book sold to qualifying organizations developing programs to prevent child abuse.

Designed by Ivy Mindlin and Amy Zimmerman
Copyright© 1991 Terry and Barbara Cecil

PeaPod Publishing, a division of Infiniti, Inc. / Atlanta, Georgia

CHRISGOPHER COLUMBUS logo and logo design are registered
trademarks for Infiniti, Inc.
ISBN: 0-9633016-0-8
Manufactured in the United Stated of America
10 9 8 7 6 5 4 3 2 1

"Chrisgopher! Didn't you hear me? Come down from there this instant!"

As Chrisgopher's daydream popped from his head, he had to grab a branch to keep from falling from his perch in the tree. "I wish I could travel to somewhere, anywhere. I like the orphanage, but I'm tired of just dreaming of adventure. I want to live it," he thought. "Yes, Mother. I'll be down in a minute."

"Chrisgopher, I need you right now, please. We are almost out of gruel, and I need you to find acorns if we are to eat tonight."

Chrisgopher called her "Mother," but then all of the orphans did, as well. He liked living at the orphanage. He could remember little of anywhere else, but he knew there must be much more out there somewhere. He was tired of eating gruel every meal, but Mother seemed to make up for the menu by giving the orphans all the love they needed and providing the best she could for them. With the exception of his adventurous spirit, Chrisgopher was not that different from any other young gopher. As he climbed down the tree, an idea burst into his head. "I know where I can get tonight's dinner," he thought. Thus, begins the adventure to forever change the world.

Chrisgopher made his way to the Royal Estate, which had always been off limits to the orphans. After burrowing underneath the wall, he stood up and glanced around the courtyard. There to his delight stood a patch of pecan trees. Chrisgopher crawled toward the trees and the precious nuts lying beneath them.

Suddenly Chrisgopher heard someone coming. Frightened for his life, he dove into a dark hole in the base of a tree. Chrisgopher trembled

with fear as he heard the voices getting louder, "Isabella, my Queen, do you really think Columbus has a chance to finding the riches we seek? Who has ever dared sail this route toward the edge of the World?"

"My dear Ferdinand, some say the risk Columbus takes will surely result in his demise, but if he is successful, our country will have the riches it desperately needs. Think of it, my King, enough gold to secure our future, and enough new foods and spices to last hundreds of years!"

Chrisgopher suddenly stopped shaking. "Enough food to last hundreds of years!" he thought. "I wish I could go on such an adventure. No one from the orphanage had ever been even this far, let alone travel on an ocean. That would save my friends in the orphanage from going hungry and having to eat that awful gruel." Chrisgopher listened to the King and Queen of Spain discuss the details of Columbus' plans to leave. He then decided he would go with Columbus on this great adventure.

Without telling anyone goodbye, he sneaked out that night to make the trek to the por of Palos de la Frontera. This is where Columbus and his ships, the Niña, the Piñta and the Santa Maria soon would be leaving on the voyage.

After many long and tedious days of travel, he finally reached Palos de la Frontera. When he found Columbus' ships, he met the many different animals that were also going on the voyage:

The pigs told him that it would be fun, and there would be lots of good food;

The sheep warned him that it would be very dangerous,

they might even fall off the edge of the Earth;
The horses thought he was too small and scared to go along;
The cows quietly wondered why any of them were leaving;
They all warned him that Christopher Columbus was out to change history. They would only refer to him as "The Admiral."

The crew started loading the animals on board, and Chrisgopher had second thoughts about going.

At the last minute and with the animals cheering through the portholes, Chrisgopher ran up the anchor rope and jumped on board.

As the Santa Maria left port, Chrisgopher crept up on deck and climbed up the main mast hoping to get his last look at his home disappearing from view. Just as he reached the crow's nest, something popped up and startled him. Chrisgopher lost his hold on the rope and plummeted toward the ocean below. Only inches away from the deep dark water, Chrisgopher was gently swooped up and carried back to the deck.

Chrisgopher was shaken and scared. But his fear turned to shock when he saw before him an old pelican with tattered feathers on his oversized wings. The pelican stood on yellow wrinkled feet that looked strained from years of holding up his plump round body. His sad eyes looked at Chrisgopher and his large drooping beak smiled at Chrisgopher in obvious delight.

8

espite the pelican's good deed, Chrisgopher frowned and asked, "Why were you hiding in the crow's nest. Don't you know better?" The pelican's feelings were visibly hurt, and the sparkle faded from his eyes. Chrisgopher knew he had been wrong to snap at this old bird, and he apologized.

Chrisgopher again asked him what he was doing in the crow's nest. The pelican said his name was Tocar, and he had traveled to lands Chrisgopher could only dream about. Tocar had heard that the Admiral was sailing to the Far East and knew that at his age this might be his last wonderful adventure. That is why he was a stowaway on the Santa Maria, just like Chrisgopher.

The long, grueling voyage took its toll on all the passengers, human and animal alike. During the voyage Chrisgopher and Tocar became good friends which helped strengthen both their spirits. It had been over forty days since they left Spain, and everyone wondered if they would ever set foot on land.

Tocar decided he had to try and find land, even if it meant he might never see his friends again.

As he turned to take off,
Chrisgopher ran over to him and
wished him good luck. Tocar had now been
gone for two days and Chrisgopher
began to worry about him.

A fog had set in, making Chrisgopher's watch difficult. All of a sudden, Tocar came flying wildly out of the mist. He landed right on Chrisgopher with a mighty thud. "You're off course! We've got to turn the ship around!" Tocar gasped. Because of the storm and the clouds, the Admiral could not see the stars to guide him. They didn't have any time to lose.

The other animals didn't believe that Tocar had actually seen land. Chrisgopher showed them the palm fronds Tocar had brought back with him. Suddenly, the door opened with a crash. The Admiral stood before them with a scowl that terrified the animals. All the other animals hid, but poor Chrisgopher wasn't fast enough.

This was the first time the Admiral had
seen Chrisgopher. How did a gopher get on
board? The Admiral started toward him,
when he realized Chrisgopher held
palm fronds in his hands. The Admiral yelled
with joy! He didn't know how, but he knew that
Chrisgopher had proof that land was near.

The Admiral bent down and took the fronds
from Chrisgopher's hands, and told them from
now on, Chrisgopher and Tocar would be his first
mates for good luck! The Admiral told
Chrisgopher he reminded
him of an old friend,
the great Italian
explorer, Amerigo
Vespucci.

The next morning the animals and the crew awoke to the yells of "Tierra! Tierra!" Land had been sighted! The whole ship rejoiced and signaled to the Piñta and the Niña. They were safe! The ships set anchor, and everyone unsteadily walked onto land. After being at sea for over forty days, they finally felt firm land beneath them.

Chrisgopher was in awe at how different this new land was from his home. After walking on the beach for awhile, he decided to explore the forest of this new world. Chrisgopher hadn't gone far, when he heard screams. He ran toward the cries for help and saw a huge green snake about to eat what appeared to be another gopher!

Thinking quickly, Chrisgopher rushed over and bit the snake's tail as hard as he could.

With a loud hiss and his fangs exposed, the snake slithered toward Chrisgopher. As the snake sprung, the gopher and Chrisgopher dove into a tree hole just in time to miss being eaten. The hole was too small for the snake, and after waiting awhile, he slithered off into the trees.

14

"Y ou saved my life," the gopher said. She was still scared, and looked at Chrisgopher curiously. "Who are you, and where did you come from?"

Chrisgopher told her about the journey and asked her name. "Pearl," she said shyly. It fit, Chrisgopher thought as he gazed at her friendly smile.

"Now that you know about me, where did you come from? And how did you get the name Pearl?" Chrisgopher asked.

"I live not far from here with my family. My father named me Pearl. He said I spend more time searching for pearls in their shells than I do looking for food."

As Pearl thanked Chrisgopher, she offered him a hard brown chunk of what looked like dried mud. Chrisgopher asked what it was. "It's chocolate, silly," she laughed, "haven't you ever eaten chocolate before?" Chrisgopher hesitantly took a bite, and immediately started smiling.

"This is excellent!" he mumbled while chewing the chocolate. "We don't have this in the Old World."

Pearl couldn't believe that where Chrisgopher came from, they didn't have any chocolate. Chrisgopher said that this new land of hers is very different from his world. He told her that they thought they were landing in the Far East, but this was a new world.

"I wonder what else our worlds have to offer each other?" Chrisgopher thought. Standing there with Pearl, he decided to call this New World, America, after the Admiral's friend, Amerigo Vespucci.

To make sure his new friend was safe, Chrisgopher walked Pearl back to her home. Pearl introduced him to her mother, father and two brothers. After hearing the frightening story, Pearl's father and mother cried as they hugged and thanked Chrisgopher for saving their daughter.

To celebrate
their new friendship
they decided to have a
feast. It would be fun trying the different foods from the New
and Old Worlds. They captivated each other for hours describing
delicious morsels soon to be discovered.

18

he next day Chrisgopher led the animals through the trees to Pearl's home. Pearl heard them coming and rounded her family together to meet them. As Chrisgopher and the animals came into their sight, Pearl and her family screamed and ran back into their home.

Chrisgopher was very confused. He went to Pearl's home and called for her. "Pearl? What's wrong?" He heard Pearl quietly ask, "Who are those strange animals with you?" Chrisgopher convinced Pearl to come out and meet his friends. One by one the horses, cows, bull, pigs, sheep, chickens and even the honeybees introduced themselves to Pearl and her family. "We've never seen animals such as these," Pearl whispered to Chrisgopher.

"You mean you don't have these animals in America?" he gasped in amazement. "I can't imagine not having any horses, or pigs, or chickens, or cows or even honeybees here!" Pearl and her family became more and more comfortable with all of the animals. "When are we going to eat?" cried the pigs.

"We are waiting for our friend Pavo, and then we can start," said Pearl's mother. As soon as the words left her mouth, a loud squawking came from the direction of the trees. Everyone watched a big round bird run toward them. Pearl told Chrisgopher that this was their friend, Pavo. This was the first time Chrisgopher and the other animals had ever seen a turkey. There weren't any turkeys in the Old World. "Let's eat!" everyone shouted.

"**S**ince you are our guests, we want you to try our foods first," Pearl told them. Pearl and her family served Chrisgopher and his friends foods from the New World they had never eaten or seen. The horses ate wild rice, potatoes and blueberries, while the cows and the bull feasted on squash and sweet potatoes.

The pigs attacked the pumpkin, pineapple and chili peppers and when they were through, ate all of the tomatoes!

The sheep snacked on green beans, lima beans and vanilla beans.

The chickens dove into the corn and cashews.

The honeybees went from the marigolds to the petunias.

There was Chrisgopher sitting in a pile of empty peanut and cashew shells. While the animals were enjoying all of their foods, Chrisgopher told them to save room for dessert. He then began to place the Old World foods in front of Pavo, Pearl, and her family. "All of these foods were brought over on the Admiral's ships, the Niña, the Pinta, and the Santa Maria. Pearl told me yesterday, these foods do not exist in the New World, America," Chrisgopher proudly stated.

"To drink we have something many of the adults drink, coffee! If you want to sweeten it, put some of this sugar cane in it and just stir," Chrisgopher said. "Since Pearl's favorite food is fruit, we brought you peaches, pears and oranges, lemons and bananas. For you, Pavo, we brought wheat, barley and oats. And for Pearl's father we have onions, cabbage, and lettuce. Pearl's mother should like both okra and olives. And for dessert, the juiciest food of them all, watermelon!"

Pavo, Pearl and her family especially enjoyed eating the watermelon, and their faces dripped with juice. It didn't take long for Pearl's brothers, the twins, to start a food fight with great big gobs of banana and watermelon.

"I can't believe we have had these wonderful delights, but I have a surprise for all of my friends," Chrisgopher said. He helped Pearl bring out giant chunks of chocolate to give to all of the animals!

Pearl's mother then asked, "Chrisgopher, how did you ever survive without chocolate?"

Everyone laughed as Chrisgopher licked chocolate from his furry face.

Pearl's father held up his cup and proposed a toast. "The discovery of these foods to both our worlds will be enjoyed for lifetimes to come."

ver the next few weeks, Chrisgopher and the animals from the Santa Maria explored the New World, America. They were homesick while they told Pearl about their home back in the Old World.

One day Chrisgopher gave Pearl some seeds. He told her that from the seeds, flowers would bloom. He hadn't seen these flowers here and knew she would love them. They are called daisies, lilacs, daffodils, and tulips. "Chrisgopher, I'll always think of you when I see these flowers."

After much time had passed, Chrisgopher heard the Admiral telling his crew that they would be sailing back to Spain within a few days. Sadness overcame Chrisgopher at the thought of leaving his new friends and America, but he was excited to be going back home to his old friends at the orphanage. Suddenly, he gasped, "Pearl!"

Chrisgopher raced to tell Pearl the sad news. He finally found her among the oysters, searching for her pearls. "Pearl, Pearl!" he shouted, "We're leaving, we're leaving!"

After he told her what he had heard, she began to gently weep. "Please stay, Chrisgopher. Live with us, your family's here now."

"But I do have a family, the orphanage. They need me, but I promise I'll be back, and soon."

"This is to help you to remember me until you get back," she said, as she pinned her prized pearl onto his hat. Chrisgopher said softly, "This pearl will be my good luck charm to ensure my safe return back to America."

Tocar decided to take a much needed rest in this New World of plenty, and promised to watch over Pearl. After all goodbyes were said, the ships finally set sail for Spain.

26

Not far from land, the Santa Maria suddenly hit a coral reef and began to sink. Chrisgopher became a hero by helping save many of the crew and animals, and even managed to save all of the food. They all continued their journey home aboard the Niña.

Everyone aboard was now confident about this trip. They knew now that the Earth wasn't flat, and they couldn't fall off the edge. The anima were especially happy, because they ha delicious foods from the New World which they could eat all the way home. And Chrisgopher had brought chunks upon chunks of his chocolate.

The Niña
and Piñta were
almost home when a violent
storm hit. As the waves crashed
down on the ship, the crew struggled to
fasten down the sails. Chrisgopher was helping
tie the ropes on the mast when a huge wave knocked
his hat into the ocean below. Chrisgopher took a deep breath
and dove head first into the waves. "Man overboard! Man overboard!" someone cried.

The crew was searching the water trying to get a glimpse of
Chrisgopher, but couldn't find him. "There he is! Get a rope to
him!" screamed the Admiral. The crew and the animals were
throwing ropes to save Chrisgopher, but the monstrous waves
kept dragging him under. It seemed hopeless, when suddenly
he was lifted into the air and pushed toward the Niña.

veryone was cheering. Chrisgopher was riding on the nose of a snow-white dolphin. Just as he reached the Niña, the dolphin tossed Chrisgopher onto the anchor rope where he was pulled to safety, still gripping his hat.

The Admiral bent over and picked up Chrisgopher in his arms. He told the crew and the animals he was giving Chrisgopher his last name, and he would now be known as Chrisgopher Columbus, Admiral of the Oceans. As everyone cheered, the Admiral and Chrisgopher were the only ones to notice that the storm had separated them from the Piñta. They were now alone on their journey home.

The next week they finally reached Palos de la Frontera. There stood all of the townspeople to welcome them home As soon as they docked, Chrisgopher said goodbye to all of his new friends. The Admiral even hugged and thanked him. Chrisgopher wanted to stay and celebrate, but he had lots of new foods to give to Mother and the rest of his friends at the orphanage. Before leaving, Chrisgoph looked out over the ocean and whispered to himself, "I'll be back soon, America." But for now, Chrisgopher Columbus was home.

THE END